My first 500 Words

I GOT THEM!

OFFSHOOT KIDS

Contents

Me
and
My Family

Hey! This is me.

hair

eyes

face

ear

nose

mouth

hand

arm

fingers

leg

foot

toes

And that's my family.

grandmother

grandfather

father

mother

aunt

uncle

brother

sister

cousins

Being with your family is a lot of fun.
Paste their pictures, miss no one.

My House

My living room

picture frame

books

bookshelf

clock

curtains

mantel

fireplace

candelabrum

vase

table lamp

sofa

cushion

chair

table

carpet

recliner

8

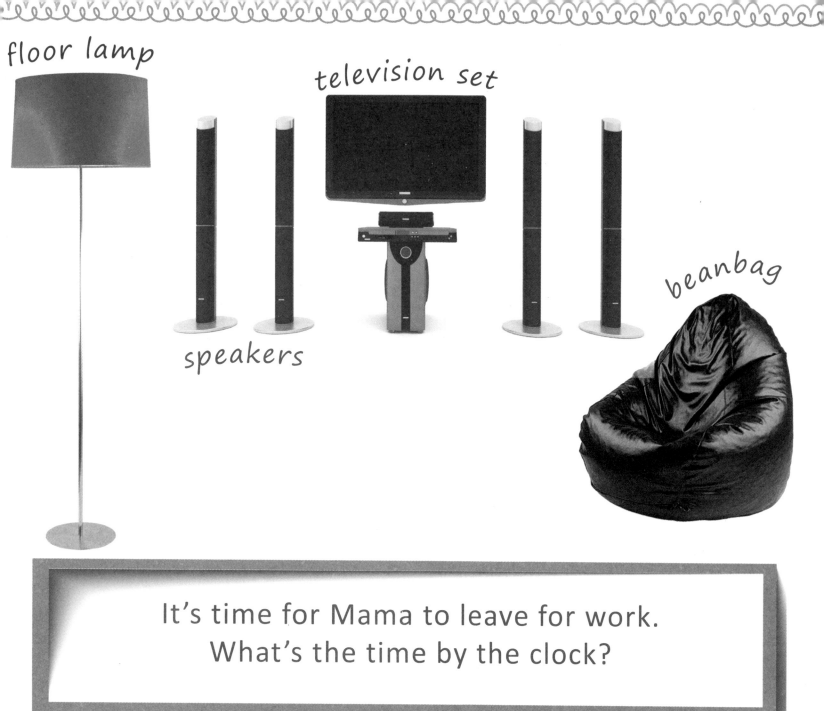

floor lamp

television set

beanbag

speakers

It's time for Mama to leave for work.
What's the time by the clock?

8 o'clock

7 o'clock

My kitchen

ladle

turner

spatula

chimney

mittens

frying pan

colander

kitchen napkin

apron

kettle

gas stove

refrigerator

oven

dishwasher

cooking range

10

chopping board

bottle opener

molds

grater

strainer

rolling pin

whisk

can opener

cleaning sponge

measuring cup

rice cooker

toaster

microwave

food processor

Look at the things lying around,
Circle the things which in the kitchen are found.

My bathroom

shower cap

shower curtain

towels

shower

mirror

bathrobe

toilet roll

sink

rubber toys

faucet

water closet

bathtub

12

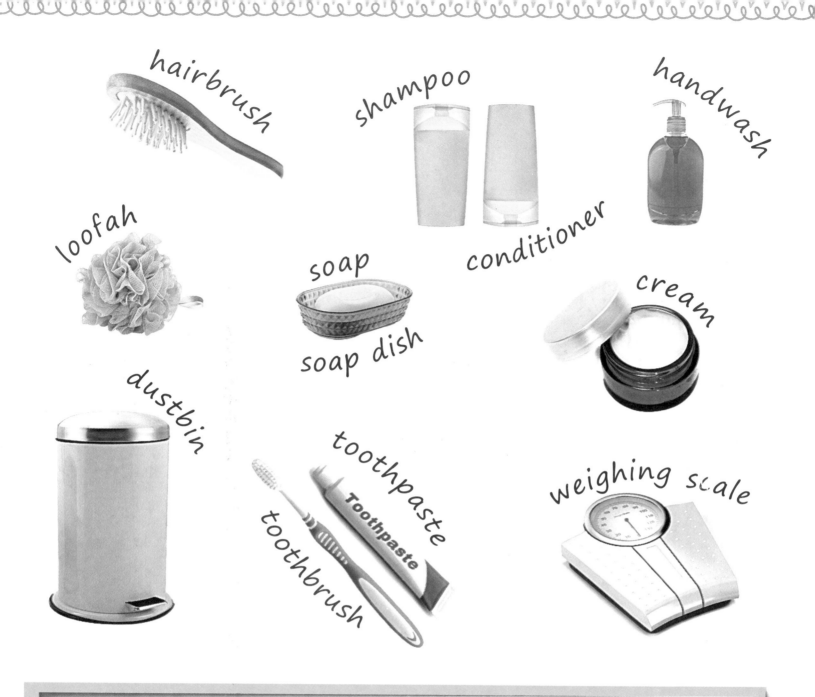

hairbrush

shampoo

handwash

loofah

soap

conditioner

soap dish

cream

dustbin

toothpaste

toothbrush

weighing scale

What would you use to wash your hands?

My bedroom

closet

table lamp

study lamp

books

study table

pillows

blanket

ottoman

rug

bed

bedsheets

duvet

dressing table

chest of drawers

Look at the pillows, soft and bright,
Color the shape that is right.

My sister's nursery

rings

diaper pins

pacifier

rocking horse

cot

ball

soft toys

walker

rattle

feeding bottle

feeding cup

chair

table

teether

high chair

baby gym

toys

Are you ready to color each teddy?

Things with Which We Fix, Clean and Mend

Things with which

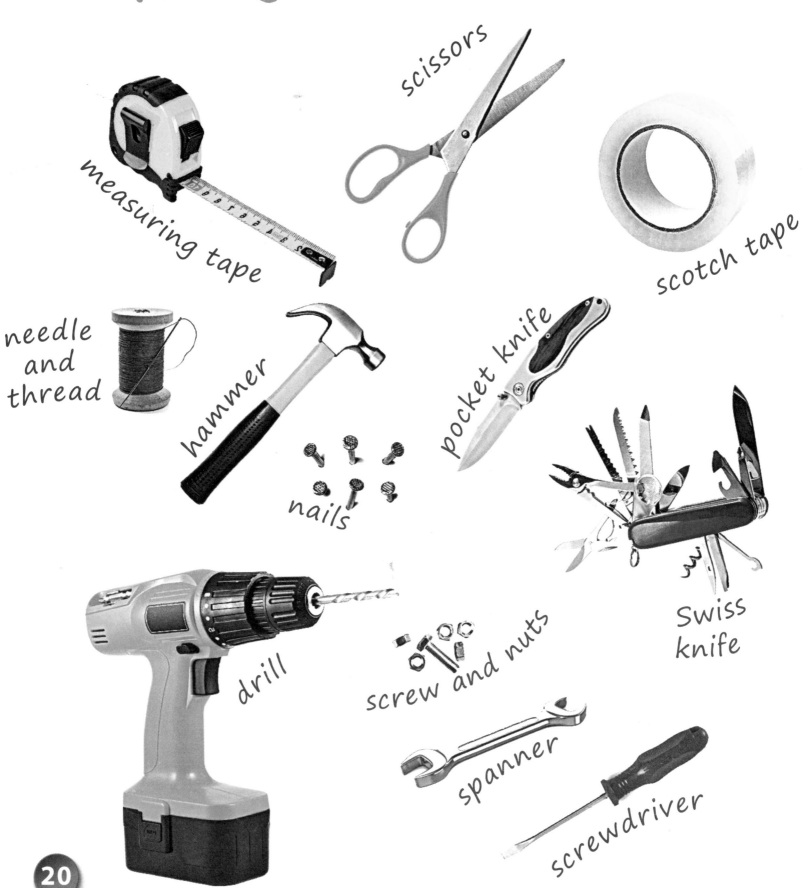

measuring tape

scissors

scotch tape

needle and thread

hammer

nails

pocket knife

Swiss knife

drill

screw and nuts

spanner

screwdriver

we fix, clean and mend

gloves

brush and dustpan

cleaning sponges

vacuum cleaner

bucket

mop

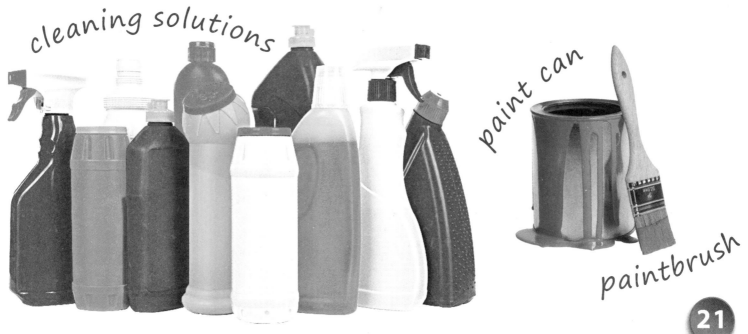

cleaning solutions

paint can

paintbrush

washing machine

laundry basket

iron

ironing board

With what can you wipe the floor?
Pup's footsteps lead to the door!

My Garden

watering can

lawn mower

fertilizer

watering pipe

bucket

wheelbarrow

My garden tools

sickle

trowel

scythe

rubber gloves

shears

seed

boots

shovel

spade

rake

axe

hoe

Flowers in my garden

primroses

peony

cosmos

viola

magnolia

buttercup

camellia

carnation

forget-me-not

daffodils

petunias

sunflower

rhododendrons

azaleas

hollyhocks

lilies

daisies

jasmine

lavenders

poppy

rose

tulips

hawthorns

Insects in my garden

cricket

ant

firefly

wasp

mosquito

cockroach

dragonfly

flea

bee

earwig

ladybug

fly

mantis

grasshopper

cicada

butterfly

moth

beetle

Some other creatures in my garden

caterpillar

scorpion

spider

snail

How a butterfly is born.

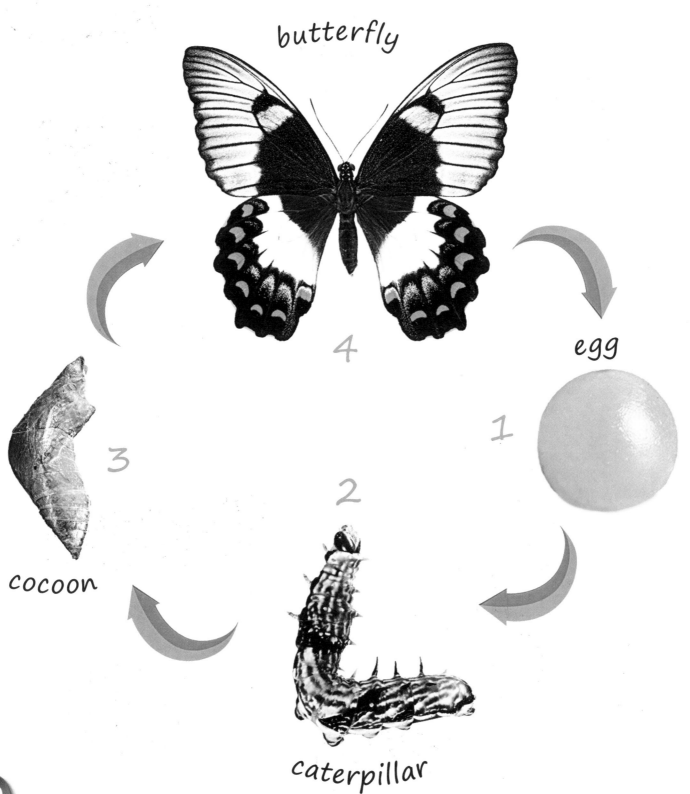

butterfly

egg

1

2

3

cocoon

caterpillar

4

My School

Things in my school

whiteboard

backpack

marker pens

felt-tip pens

paint brushes

highlighter pens

poster paints

crayons

palette

color pencils

set square

protractor

ruler

pencil pouch

compass

gluestick

sharpener

pen

erasers

pencils

tape dispenser

sipper

books

lunch box

desk

chair

In your schoolbag, what would you not keep?

Food I Eat

Vegetables I eat

broccoli

cauliflowers

cabbage

potatoes

tomato

mushrooms

corns

eggplant

bell peppers

okra

celery

scallion

spinach

squash

onion

garlic

ginger

cucumber

carrot

radish

lettuce

zucchini

beans

avocados

asparagus

lemon

peas

turnip

kale

beet

chilies

spices

Fruits I eat

pomegranates

grapes

banana

melon

nectarine

guava

cherries

kiwi

apple

orange

watermelon

blackberries

mango

peaches

plum

blueberries

apricot

pineapple

raspberries

papaya

coconut

strawberries

pear

39

Meals that I eat

bacon and eggs

cheese

sandwich

donuts

croissant

cereal

fruit salad

bagels

pancakes and syrup

waffles

sausages

pork ribs

goulash

dinner rolls

chips and dip

steak

fish and chips

wrap

sushi

salad

soup

pork and beans

pizza

noodles

pasta

shepherd's pie

ice creams

milk shake

juices

Color the burger, it's yum.
Don't eat it alone, share with mum.

fork   knife

spoon

coaster

salt shaker

table napkin

pepper shaker

cup

saucer

jug

glass

plate

bowl

dining table

place mat

Seasons
I Love

Seasons

Spring	Summer	Autumn	Winter
flowers	bright	yellow	cold
bloom	sunny	fall	snowy
green	warm	dry leaves	white

Clothes I wear

T-shirt

frocks

capri pants

skirt

sandals

shades

cap

jumpsuit

top

Bermuda shorts

shorts

My beach vacation

beach umbrella

sunscreen

towels

spades

deck chair

bucket

beach ball

sunglasses

swimsuit

floating tube

swimming trunks

surfboards

sandcastle

flip-flops

seashell

sand

Winter clothes

jumper

cap

scarf

jacket

coat

jeans

socks

gloves

boots

shoes

My winter vacation

snowflakes

ski suit

snowball

skis

ice skates

sled

ski gloves

helmet

ski goggles

snowmobile

It's sunny and hot—what clothes have you got?

Special Days
I Celebrate

balloons

waffles

candies

jellies

chips

muffins

cupcakes

chocolates

birthday cake

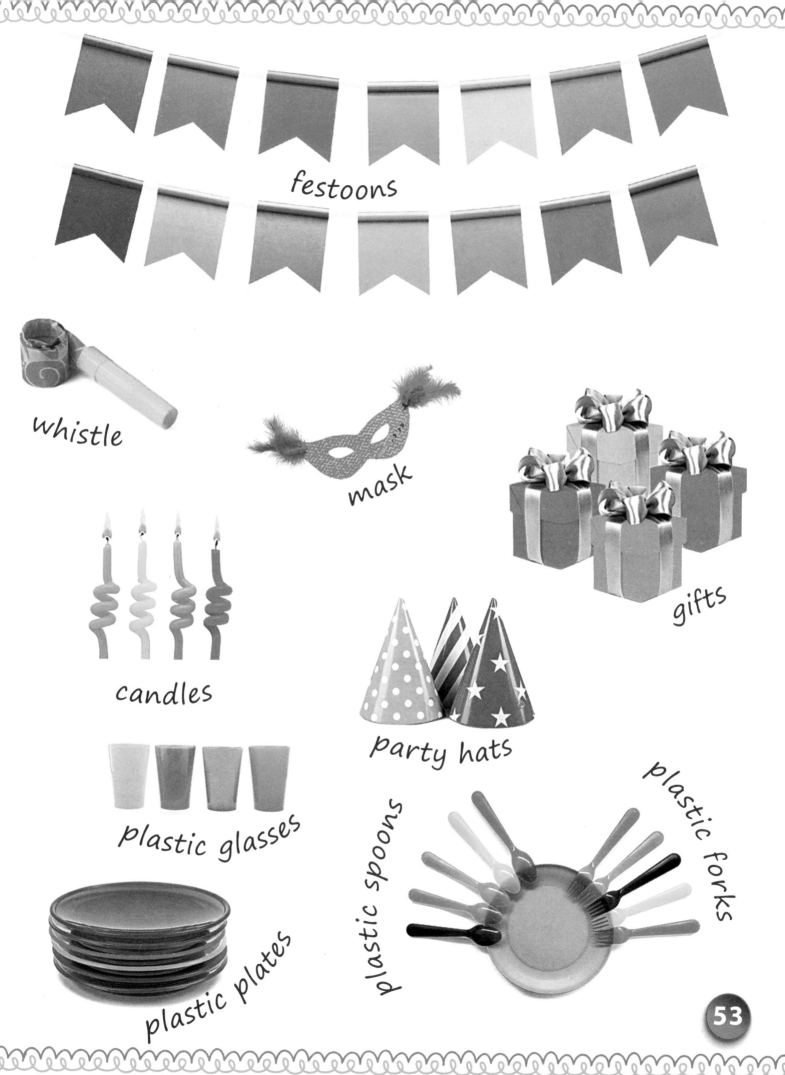

festoons

whistle

mask

gifts

candles

party hats

plastic glasses

plastic plates

plastic spoons

plastic forks

53

My Halloween celebration

ghost

mask

jack-o'-lantern

pumpkin

scarecrow

witch

cape

elves

My holiday celebrations

snowman

hat

gifts

ornaments

Santa Claus

reindeers

holly

Christmas tree

stocking

plum cake

gingerbread cookies

bells

candy canes

fairy lights

57

Where does Santa leave gifts for you?

Transport We Use

Things that move on land

motor bike

fire engine

car

train

InterCity EXPRESS

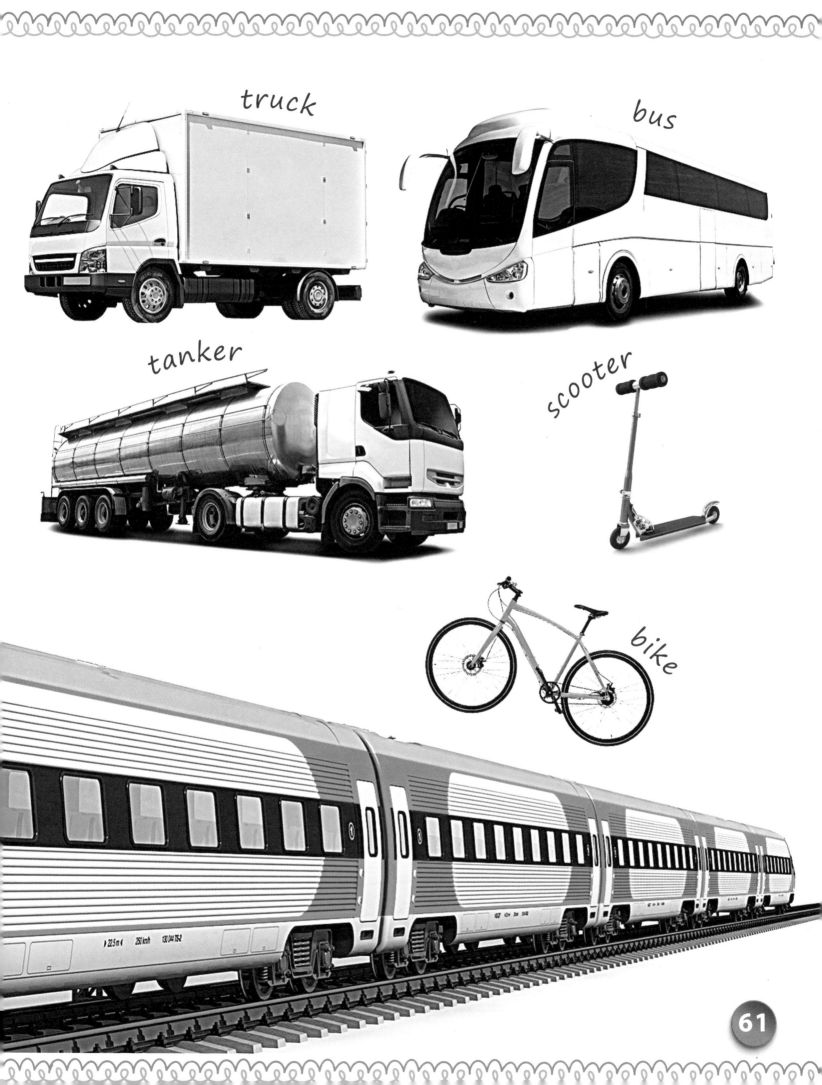

truck

bus

tanker

scooter

bike

Things that move in air

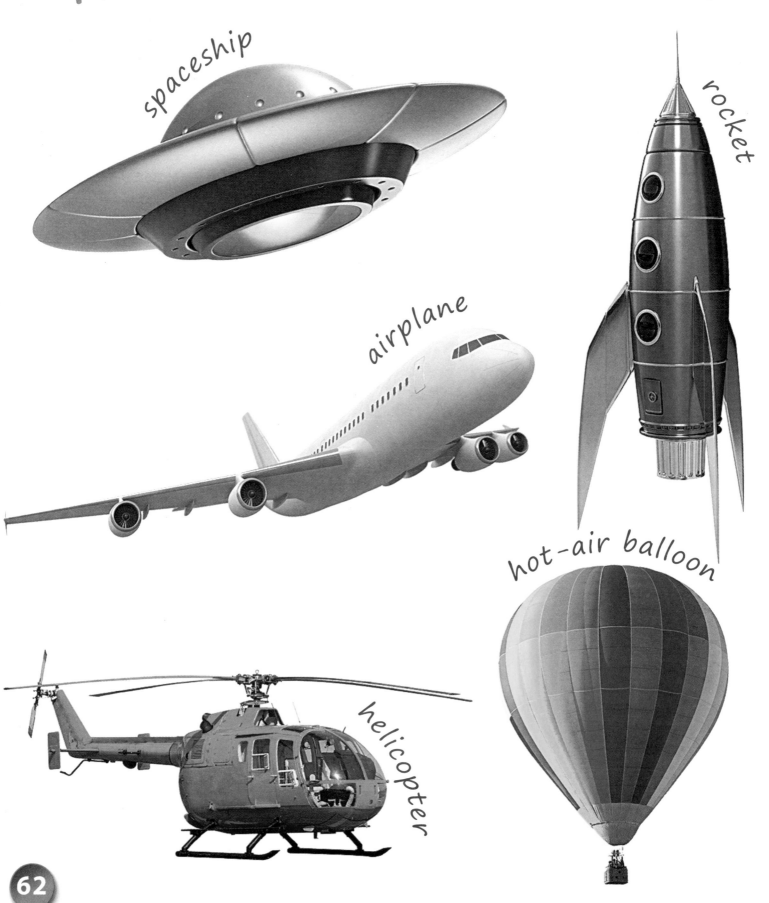

spaceship

rocket

airplane

hot-air balloon

helicopter

Things that move in water

kayak

row boat

canoe

raft

submarine

cargo ship

yacht

cruise ship

This is what aliens travel in,
Can you mark and draw a twin?

Animals Around Us

Pet animals

mouse

hamster

cat

parrot

rabbit

goldfish

turtle

dog

What would you keep in this bowl?
Circle in a second, that's your goal.

Farm animals

pig

donkey

sheep

goat

cow

horse

rooster

hen

duck

turkey

goose

It moves on two legs.
Which of these gives us eggs?

Animals in the zoo

camel

kangaroo

zebra

porcupine

giraffe

elephant

leopard

fox

wolf

tiger

monkey

panther

snake

bear

lion

Animals in water

shark

dolphin

seal

octopus

lobster

whale

alligator

squid

starfish

prawn

jellyfish

otter

turtle

fish

hippopotamus

crab

73

Birds

eagle

frigate

owl

cormorant

vulture

swan

albatross

ostrich

quail

peacock

pigeon

partridge

swallow

kingfisher

robin

woodpecker

seagull

sparrow

penguin

stork

Animal babies

lamb

kitten

fawn

duckling

chick

piglet

kid

puppy

foal

cub

calf

Colors
Around Us

Colors I know

green

red

yellow

blue

orange

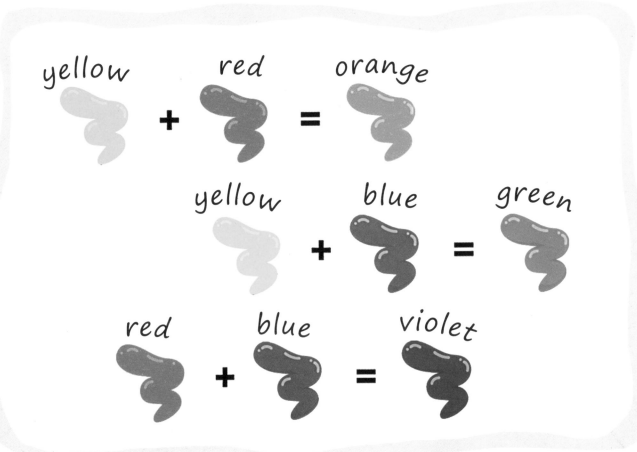

yellow + red = orange

yellow + blue = green

red + blue = violet

Let's play a game.
All you need to do is color them the same!

Shapes Around Us

Shapes I know

This is a rectangle.

Shapes around me

This is a triangle.

This is a circle.

This is a square.

A different color for each name.
Choose the right shape, color it, that's your aim!

star

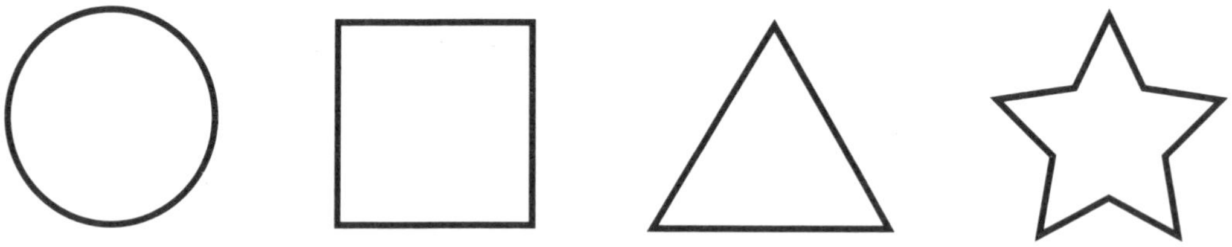

square

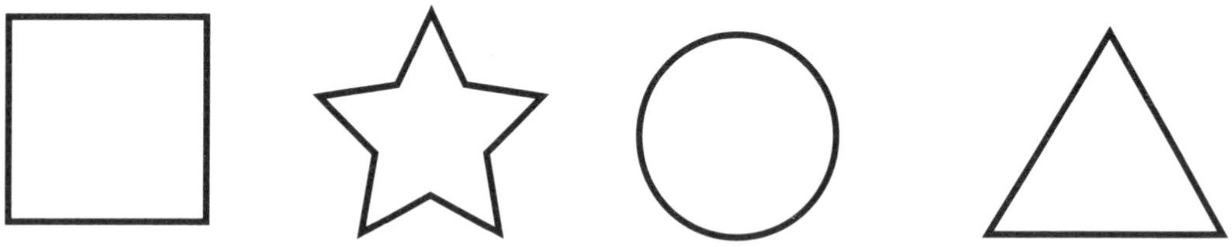

triangle

circle

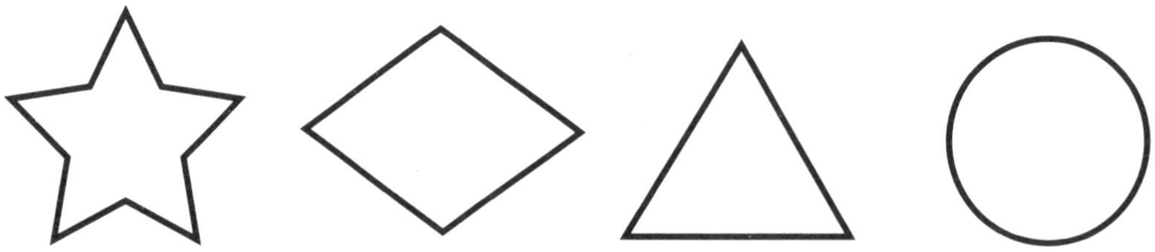

Months
and Days

Months in a year

January

February

March

April

May

June

July

August

September

October

November

December

Days in a week

 Monday

 Tuesday

 Wednesday

 Thursday

 Friday

 Sunday

 Saturday

Your timetable

Numbers
I Can Count

Numbers

one

two

three

four

five

six

seven

eight

nine

ten

Ordinal

first third fifth

second fourth

numbers

seventh

ninth

sixth

eighth

tenth

Tahitian

English

Chinese

Japanese

Scottish

Saudi Arabian

we stand

man   Indian   Mexican

Canadian   Dutch   French

My practice page

Words I have learned